A Kalmus Classic Edition

Robert

SCHUMANN

ALBUM LEAVES

Opus 124

Edited according to manuscripts and
from her personal recollections by
CLARA SCHUMANN

FOR PIANO

K 03899

Kalmus

Albumblätter
20 Klavierstücke

Album leaves
20 Pianoforte pieces

Feuilles d'Album
20 Pièces pour piano

Frau Alma von Wasielewski zugeeignet

Impromptu

Robert Schumann, Op. 124
(1832-1845)

Sehr schnell M. M. 𝅗𝅥 = 116
Assai presto

PRINTED IN U.S.A.

Leides Ahnung

Presage of Sorrow   Pressentiment triste

Langsam M. M. ♩ = 69   (1835)

Scherzino

Rasch M. M. ♩. = 100

Presto

(1832)

3

Walzer

Waltz Valse

(1835)

Phantasietanz

Fantastic Dance. Danse fantastique

Sehr rasch M. M. ♩= 104 (1836)

Assai presto

5

Wiegenliedchen

Little Cradle Song Berceuse

Nicht schnell M. M. ♩= 116
Non presto

(1843)

Ländler

Country Dance Tyrolienne

Sehr mäßig M. M. 𝅗𝅥. = 56 (1836)

Assai moderato

7

Leid ohne Ende

Grief without end Douleur sans fin

Langsam M. M. 𝅘𝅥 = 84 (1837)

Lento

8

Leidenschaftlicher
Più appassionato
Erstes Tempo
Tempo I

Impromptu

Mit zartem Vortrag M. M. ♩= 84 (1838)

Teneramente

9

Walzer

Waltz Valse

Mit Lebhaftigkeit M. M. ♩ = 168 (1838)

Con vivacità

10

Romanze

Romance Romance

Burla

Presto M.M. ♩ = 170 (1832)

Larghetto

M. M. ♩. = 54

(1832)

13

Vision

Sehr rasch M. M. ♩. = 126
Molto presto

(1838)

14

Walzer

Waltz Valse

(1832)

15

Schlummerlied
Slumber Song   Berceuse

(1841)

Allegretto M.M. ♩. = 63

im Tempo
in tempo
p
Ped.
(52)
p
p
pp
mf

pp
(molto) p
Ped.
(p)
ritard.

im Tempo
in tempo
(rit.)
(dolce)
(a tempo)
(dim.)
(ppp)
Ped.

Elfe

The Elf Sylphe

So rasch als möglich M. M. 𝅗𝅥 = 100
Il più presto possibile

(1835)

17

Botschaft

A message   Message

Mit zartem Vortrag M.M. ♩ = 152   (1838)

Teneramente

18

Phantasiestück

Fantastic Piece   Morceau de fantaisie

Leicht, etwas graziös M. M. ♩= 76
Leggero e un poco grazioso

(1839)

p (a tempo)
sf
ritard.
im Tempo
in tempo
Ped.
fp
sfp
(rit.)

Kanon

Canon Canon

*) Der Herausgeber schlägt folgende Änderung vor:
The editor suggests the following alteration:
L'éditeur propose la variante suivante:

Kalmus